Writing 29

DALE HERD

Early Morning Wind
and Other Stories

Four Seasons Foundation

Bolinas: 1972

Library of Congress Catalog Card No.: 74-166134

SBN: 0-87704-019-2

Cover photograph by E. L. Smith

Manufactured in the United States of America

FIRST EDITION

Four Seasons Foundation books are distributed by Book People,
2940 Seventh Street, Berkeley, California 94710

to

Sara Jean

"... gone down that American river."

ALLEN GINSBERG

Contents

One

Eric

She had a kid asleep in the bedroom. I asked her if she wanted to ball and she said yes. She got her gun six times. I told her I was selling my car and all my belongings and buying a sailboat and sailing to Australia. I said she could go but she'd have to pay. How much she said. A dollar thirty seven I said. She said not bad. Then she said how much for Eric. I said ten thousand dollars.

Safe

We were swimming in Lake Washington down by
the freeways. It was a beauty day, warm, easy,
gentle. The freeways were solemn, like monuments,
huge, motionless, silent, their many concrete pilings
pale grey in the sunlight, the water out from
their flanks blue on top like inverted sky then green
then brown, calm. Jeff saw some kids dive from the top
of the blocked-off freeway entrance across the lagoon
and he swam over to try it. I watched him go, arm
over arm, stirring up the surface. When he
reached the abutment just above the water he pulled
himself up, waved at me to come across. I launched
off doing a few fast butterflies, the cold shocking me for
a moment, then went on my side, gliding, and began
sidestroking, the water buoyant, bright. As I came
near the landing Jeff yelled at me.

"What's that?" I asked, grabbing onto the edge
of the concrete. It felt warm.

"Ha," Jeff grinned. I grinned back. He turned
and boosted himself up onto a ledge just below the
top of the freeway. I pulled myself out of the water,
then sat, dangling my legs, looking back across to

the lawn where our women were sitting. Coming toward me was a blue hulled kaiak, the paddler carefully stroking on one side, then on the other. I looked up in time to see Jeff balancing on the railing, then jumping off, arms out, a tall waterspout shooting up as he hit. The kaiak glided up and I gave the paddler a hand, steadying the boat while he got out to rest. Jeff surfaced and began swimming over. The kaiaker's name was Jan. He was a third year law student at the U, taking a break from studying for the bar exams. We talked for a moment about kaiaking, something I'd never done.

"It's a good sport," he said, "if you like to compete. There aren't too many guys in it and you can go a long way."

He asked me what I did. I told him Jeff and I both had just quit our jobs and were out scrambling. He took that thought in without making any comment and then said he sure hoped he passed the exams, he wanted to be maybe a government lawyer for a time then go into private practice, that way he'd get his feet on the ground and make enough solid contacts so that when he set out on his own he'd know his way around. I took a good look at him as he talked, a massive face, short hair, brown eyes, the big middle-aged thick body under the kid's skin. I figured him to move slowly getting back into the kaiak and he did, being careful not to tip himself over. I held it for him until he got the paddle ready and pushed himself off.

5

Jeff and I watched for a while. The future lawyer wasn't too good. The kaiak moved forward in jerks, not gliding out smoothly like others I'd seen. He had explained to me that kaiaks have no keel and aren't flat on the bottom — they turn over on a whim. He didn't look like any kind of competitor.

"How come you didn't dive off?" I asked Jeff. "It isn't that high."

"Didn't know how deep it was. Didn't want to break my neck, right?"

"Sure," I answered.

"I didn't see you up there," Jeff said.

Seduction and Cuckoldry

Frank and Geno were new friends. Frank had just started in the office and Geno began taking him to lunch. They would eat in the University District in order to watch the girls walking to and from school. Watching the girls was much more fun than was eating but each watched for a different reason.

Frank was newly married and he was shy about his wife. When he was alone with her he found it hard to approach her. Looking at other girls excited him and if he became excited enough he could go home and forget his shyness. He felt guilty about it but it worked.

Geno, however, had been married for five years and shyness was not his problem. He was seriously thinking of leaving his wife and looking at new lovely girls encouraged his desire for freedom.

After a few lunch hours together Geno began telling Frank some of his personal problems, problems that Frank didn't like.

Geno admitted to playing around. And while it made him seem wild and free, things Frank believed a man should be, he distrusted Geno for it and was more than a little frightened by him.

On their fourth noon hour together Frank and Geno were inside a sandwich shop watching the girls walk by. It was a bright spring day and they were talking about getting free of their jobs.

Both agreed life was too short to work for someone else. Geno said quitting might be the final straw for Jackie. Frank said his worry was the other way around.

"If I quit Betty might leave me."

"Good," Geno said. "Why not."

"What do you mean?" Frank laughed.

'You'll be free then," Geno said.

"Sure," Frank said; yet he felt threatened. Recently there had been times when he found himself wondering if Betty ever thought sexually about Geno.

"I don't want other women," Frank said.

"Maybe not," said Geno. "You never know."

"I don't," Frank emphasized. "Why do you?"

"I really don't know what I want."

"Maybe you're just looking for an escape."

"Maybe," Geno smiled. "It is funny, though. I never like the girls I get."

"Really?" Frank said.

"They either kiss wrong or they smell bad or something is wrong with them. I'll say that for Jackie; she's certainly a clean girl."

Frank laughed.

"But the real thing is," Geno said, "is that I feel

bad afterwards and I start acting good to Jackie and she responds and things go nicely for a time."

"I see," Frank said, sitting back. He had been listening intently. Two nights before he and Betty had eaten out with Geno and Jackie for the first time. They had just met Jackie and while they were waiting for the meal Geno said, Do you know what Jackie was doing when I came home? She was talking to herself in the mirror. Betty had laughed sympathetically, saying she often did the same thing. But Jackie had flared, saying, Do you know what Geno does? He poops in his shorts! Frank had been startled. He had looked at Geno. Geno hadn't flinched. Geno gently explained that Jackie had been rehearsing for a speech class. But Jackie stayed angry throughout the meal. Talking afterward Frank and Betty had agreed the outburst was unbelievable. Frank said he had been very impressed with Geno's calm. Betty said I don't see how they got married. But now, Frank felt, Geno's calm wasn't impressive. It was based on deception. He saw that Jackie wasn't entirely to blame.

"Your wife seems nice," Geno said. "You've got a good thing there."

"Thank you," Frank said.

"I'd like to start a new thing," said Geno. "I really would. I guess the only thing to do is break up. These other women aren't the thing. The real thing is my guilt. I get to feeling so bad I can't even function. I mean after a while I get so bad I can't even make it with anybody!"

"No kidding!" Frank said. "Does Jackie know you play around?"

"God, no!" Geno said. "Never arm a woman! But never!"

"No?"

"No!"

"Why not?" asked Frank.

"Because they'll use it against you," Geno said. "Just like the other night when Jackie came out with that shorts and shit thing."

"Really," Frank said, sitting back again. He was amazed.

"I could have killed her," Geno said.

"Really," Frank repeated, talking almost to himself. "Are you going to leave her?"

"Maybe," Geno said. "I don't know."

"Well," said Frank, "if you need a place to stay you can always put up at our place. We have an extra bed."

"Good," said Geno. "Fine."

The rest of the lunch hour Frank paid no attention to the girls. He thought only about how Geno really was inside. He could hardly wait to tell Betty. Men were nothing inside, he thought. They were just like babies. Frank was more excited than if he had been looking at the girls.

Geno, however, did look at the girls. And the more he looked the more he began thinking about

Betty. She really was nice, he thought, but hell, Frank was his friend.

Twins

Jenny, her body still heavy and swollen, was sitting with Beth at the kitchen table. Down the hall in the living room I could see the two pink bassinets.

"I'm not kidding," Jenny was saying, "her mind is just going wacky since I've had the twins. She's making me so damn nervous . . ."

"Take it easy," Beth said.

"Who?" I asked.

"Grandma," Beth said.

"Do you know what she did yesterday?" said Jenny. "She sat in the living room and cried because Hill didn't say hello to her and she thought that meant no one wanted her here. Mother had to give her an alcohol rub and put her to bed like a baby. She's mother's baby now; isn't that funny?"

"It's her age," Beth said. "Her arteries are hardening."

"No," Jenny said, "it's simply attention. Since the twins came she's simply not getting enough attention. She makes me so damn mad! She hasn't even once asked to hold them! Not Once!"

"I think I'll go take a look," I said.

I went down the hall into the living room. The

babies were asleep, one on its stomach, its tiny fists clenched, the other on its back, its little eyes wrinkled like an old woman's.

As I came back in the kitchen Jenny wanted to know what I thought.

"They're perfect," I said. "You're a lovely girl."

She smiled and brushed the hair back off her face. Beth gave me a wink.

Happy Dreams

About a week before Celia called, saying, "Well, we did it; I finally feel like a woman again . . ." Leaning over, a good lovely look on his face, telling us this shortly after visiting Celia and Gene for his first look at the new babies, Willy said: "Christ, seeing her nurse those twins really did it to me. The first time I ever saw anyone nurse it was twins. I was settling a route dispute in this guy's home, having a beer in the kitchen, and the guy's wife came in, sat down, lifted out her breasts and started nursing two babies just like that. My God, I wanted to knock them off and plunge in there myself. Seeing Celia do the same thing was just a bit too much. Beautiful women should know better."

We laughed. Right after that Willy left to visit his girl and Gerri called and told Celia the story. Celia laughed and said, "Yes, but did he like the babies?" Gerri laughed and said, "He didn't say but doesn't that turn you on? How long has it been? It's been more than three months now, hasn't it?

14

Hasn't Gene complained?" "Oh, no," Celia answered, "you know Gene."

Then three days later Celia called, using merrily those special sister to sister tones, not talking about her babies, saying this to Gerri: "My God, Ger, the dream I had! I don't believe it! Promise you won't tell? Ever? Promise! It's about Willy. Yes! Remember what you told me? God! Yes! We were all sitting at the table, you, me, Phil, Gene. I was feeding the twins watching you guys play bridge and Willy was under the table. Yes! No! No one knew. And all I had on was a housecoat! No! Nothing else. And he started kissing my legs! Yes! No! Yes, I did like it but I couldn't keep my face still! I was scared to death Gene would look up and see my face and Willy kept kissing higher and higher . . . it was simply . . . no . . . yes . . . ha ha ha . . ."

Ripped

The Cedars was a downhome, funky bar, Swan,
Moody, Mick the Hillbilly, Dead Ed, Donna, going
back was always fun. It was out in Ballard, out in
the old industrial section with traintracks crossing the
streets, concrete underpasses, past wrecking yards,
junkshops, old hotels for old men. We were always
stoned enroute and the twenty minute ride from the
U district could take light years but was always all right.
Duc was blowing harp out there and to see him was
always fun. Swan would take things down into
the crowd, he didn't dig the leader of the band trip
so he would jump down off the stage out of the colors
and ask everyone to shout or stomp or move. First you
were moving and then sweating and things would start
mixing in and mixing out and going on the same,
hands, head, hair, hips, up on the stage into the
lights there cupping the harp to the mike you could
really lay it out, putting it all into pulling it out
straight up from under you, feeling yourself pulling
the power from the floor, the concrete, the ground,
the earth, all of it coming up and out into everybody,
into everywhere, Swan laying it on with you, Moody

16

the same, Moody constant, always happy, you happy
sweating, everyone happy, everyone going on in
everybody, and so it would go, anyone could get up
there, most of us did, but the place was always empty
of regular customers, the management didn't dig
Swan's band so when he'd do something similar,
anything, play with his teeth, or let American Man run
on out the full set, never giving the dancers a break,
they'd threaten to can the whole group, they wanted
a straight country-western shitkicking beer outfit
in there but they weren't making enough money
to pay for it so they were stuck with Swan. The place
was nearly always empty until we got there, all our
own crowd, all the dropouts, fuckups, longhairs,
dopefiends, all us white niggers, all getting it on,
it was always a hell of a good time, no one ever got
busted, some of us even got laid out of there, picking
up some of the local stuff, Buc, in particular, Buc
had a great time with two of the local hogs, two
peroxide tipped chicks that wanted his body so he took
them on outside in Moody's Chevrolet, everyone
walked outside and looked at the steamed-over
windows.

Two

Dark

Inside the light was muted and my eyes took time
to adjust. We scuffled around for a while getting
into some sort of formal arrangement and Hugh started
into the business. Behind the girl the mother stood in
a dark blue dress, hands on her daughter's shoulders.
She wasn't staying long, she said, only until
Wednesday or perhaps Thursday, whenever Elizabeth
was calmed. Elizabeth was a nice name for the girl
and I watched her. Like the house she seemed sound
and old fashioned and solid. The light was soft on
her face and she wore no makeup and her hair was
tied straight back. She spoke in a gentle voice, a
low, even voice, and as she answered Hugh's questions
she held her hands quietly on her lap, but what she
said didn't match up and I watched her carefully,
hearing her repeat several times that she was allright,
would be allright, she could assure us about that,
and then as the questioning went on I watched her slip
away in her mind, her eyes not tracking anymore
but staying fixed, her face not changing expression,
even though her voice went on giving out the yes's
and no's that Hugh required. When this was over

and she and the mother left the room to get the baby I said shock. Hugh shook his head. I got up and went over to her empty chair.

"Flat affect," Hugh said, emphasizing the first syllable of affect. "Are you familiar with it?" Looking past him I could see the chair and my reflection in the kitchen window. "She won't respond to anything. It's a common defense mechanism in these situations."

'My ass,' I thought, looking at him. 'Was that true though? It was true of him certainly, he could certainly handle things verbally, could always find those good old categories.'

"Well," I said.

He put his finger to his lips.

The mother and the girl were coming in behind me. I walked back to my chair and sat down. The girl showed Hugh the baby, rocking it back and forth in her arms. It was just beginning to wake and looked unhappy. "Good," Hugh said, "a he or a she?" "A he," the girl said. The mother looked at me and said, "He was a wonderful boy, so bright, but he just couldn't accept the fact that other people don't always feel things the same way he does. He would just get furious."

"Did he hit anyone?" Hugh asked.

"No, he'd just beat on the wall. He'd stand over there by the refrigerator and pound on the wall. You can see the marks."

"He didn't hit anyone?"

"Oh, no."

"Who called the sheriff?"

"Elizabeth did."

The girl was sitting down again and Hugh said, "Well, let's hope he gets help, I'm sure he will." The girl didn't respond and Hugh waited a moment and then said, "Well, now if you need anything, or if something comes up, or there is some problem, you give us a call." I waited a moment and then stood up, watching the girl nod in response, and went to the door.

Outside again the sunlight was brilliant, warm. I took a deep breath. Far away over the woods there was rain, grey streaks washing down from grey clouds, all coming slowly south. The grass was wet from an earlier shower and over against the pines was a stand of young thorn trees, thin and delicate looking, with tiny, countless, fresh looking leaves.

"There," Hugh said. "I don't know if you spotted it when we pulled in." He pointed to a tall, narrow, half-painted blue, aluminium tower rising high above the garage. Steel guywires ran out from various crossbraces to stakes in the ground.

"What's that mean?"

"That he did a lot of talking. He could reach anyplace in the world, Africa, Australia, Europe, Asia."

"How about her?"

"What do you mean?"

"Could he talk to her?"

"Good question," Hugh said, looking at me. It was a hostile look, probably in response to how I was talking. He was sensing I thought him an ass. Maybe he wasn't.

We got in the car. I rolled down the window and looked at the house, old farmhouse, blind man's home. It looked deserted and abstract. Why had she married him. She was educated. So was Hugh. So was I. So what did that mean.

"Unhappy," Hugh said, "desperately unhappy." He was saying something else but his head was turned watching back along the car as we started backing out of the driveway.

I looked back at the house again, imagining how it had been built, wondering if friends had come together giving each other their time, all of them working on what had to be done, that would have been over seventy years ago, now nothing there, no sign of life, only an aesthetic, pure white against the dark green of the woods.

"Some kind of will to fail," Hugh said. He braked the car, then started us out in a curve, getting us on the road. "He brought her out here where he knew he couldn't get work. No one out here has work for him. Did I tell you what the psychiatric summary said about this?"

"No," I said, and he went on, I could hear some words he was saying as I watched down the road, seeing the trees on the sides narrow down to a solid mass of dark greygreen, finding myself thinking about Northern State Hospital, thinking about the rooms there, trying to get it right in my mind, seeing the girl going in there for the first time, seeing her going down the long narrow corridors, all well lit and empty, the light reflecting around in a glare, the floors polished and hard, the white walls. Outside it was lovely, a winding road between broad lawns and very old trees. As you came up toward the buildings, the buildings handsome and calm to look on, away in the longish distance far past the trees would be the deep blue of the Cascades going away north unbroken as far as you could see, the air fresh and clean,

"Well," Hugh said, "what do you think?"

"I don't know," I said.

Out the window was a Phillips 66 station, a long, empty field behind the asphalt apron, then trees. A sudden blast of rain blurred the windshield. Hugh turned on the wipers.

"I thought you would find that interesting," he said.

Joy

When we were sixteen Jack and I were best friends.
He was a dark haired, heavy-set kid and had a car,
a 1948 Plymouth. That summer I was a sexual
innocent. Jack had a job at the produce house sacking
carrots. After work he'd drive by and pick me up.
He had a fat girl friend named Joy who bleached her
hair. The three of us would cruise around together in
the evenings.

One night Jack came by late. Joy was sitting
tight against him. She didn't answer me when I said
hello. "Wow," I said, "what's that smell? It really
smells rotten in here." "What smell?" Jack said. "Wow,"
I said. I rolled down the window and stuck my head
out as we started off. No inkling of what that rank
and powerful smell was crossed my mind.

I remember feeling strong and romantic that
evening, riding along the town streets with my head
out the window, keeping myself away from the press
and reek of whatever it was inside the car's darkness,
feeling remarkably clearheaded, knowing Jack's
girl was really a slut and he didn't know it.

Old Hotels

His wife left him back in 1950 and he never got
over it. He cooked at the hotel where I bellhopped and
everytime he got paid he'd go out and buy T-bones
and cook two and give me one. He drank all the
time and everytime he got drunk he'd say the same
things over and over. "Lets see if you can name all
the teams in the Big Ten. Lets see if I can do it. I can
do it." He never did. He'd always leave one out. He'd
say, "Did I say Ohio, the Ohio Buckeyes? Did I?"
 He had bad congestion and coughed all the time.
The drinking made it worse. He drank beer in the
head and after his shift he'd be drunk and want me
to go with him in the elevator. The motion of the
elevator made him sick and phlegm would dribble out
his mouth. Then he'd want me to go to his room.
He didn't like being alone there. Everytime I'd go up
with him in the elevator I'd end up putting him to
bed, clothes and all. No matter which way you laid him,
face up or face down, he'd put his hands on his crotch
and start hunching. If I started to leave he'd begin
to cry. I'd have to sit with him until he fell asleep.

Captain Baa Baa

When the first contingent of American troops
withdrawn from Viet Nam comes home in the summer
of 69 at McChord Air Force Base General Richard
C. Williamson, former Commander in Chief in Viet
Nam and then current Army Chief of Staff, is there to
greet two-ninths of them with a handshake.

For many of these men (all sharp looking, all deeply
tanned, all wearing highly polished combat boots
and clean combat fatigues, sleeves rolled to the
bicep), certainly for those who wear a small round
button in their lapel that reads We Try Harder,
the slogan of Avis Rent-A-Car, America's second
leading car rental agency, the greeting by Williamson,
the highest ranking officer they have ever seen, is
particularly memorable.

Standing tall, every inch the picture of the nation's
top general, wearing no extra insignia save the gold
and silver braid on the glossy brim of his high crowned
hat, the four silver stars on each collar of his summer
dress blouse and a single blue infantryman's badge
over his left breast pocket, Williamson's firm grip,
six foot one inch height, and rugged face of hard

jawline, lean cheeks and massive black eyebrows accent his position of command and lend power to the solemnity of the occasion.

And when, giving the last address of the afternoon to the entire contingent of 814 men, the sun hammering at his face, occasionally ricocheting off his stars, but never affecting his eyes, eyes protected by shadow cast from the brim of his hat, his bearing, to every man there, reinforces the words he speaks:

"I want to convey to you the appreciation of our nation — appreciation for a job well done.

"You have grown and developed while you have been in uniform. You will find yourself more mature, more dedicated to the service of others, more responsible, more realistic and more practical than your contemporaries who have not served.

"You have served while others stood by, and talked, and demonstrated.

"But, of course, you have demonstrated too.

"You have demonstrated your responsibility by doing your duty for your country.

"Those who stay in the Army will benefit from your experience in Viet Nam."

Earlier in the day shortly before the contingent lands in the nine silver C-141 transports Williamson presides over another ceremony. Hatless this time but, as later, not seeming to look anywhere but straight ahead, surrounded by aides, base officers, their aides, doctors, military and civilian newsmen and photographers, Williamson walks through the wards of Madigan General Hospital and decorates six of the wounded already home from Viet Nam.

For five of the men, all enlisted men, the hospital staff has made the normal frantic pre-inspection preparations: clean bedding put on all beds; walls, windows, woodwork and floors washed; all tables, chairs, food trays, crash-carts, bedpans and urinals, books, magazines, newspapers and personal effects hidden away under beds and shoved into closets; each man given his personal uniform, cleaned and pressed, complete with rank and insignia.

The sixth man, a twenty-five year old Captain, presented a special problem. Struck by a Viet Cong mortar fragment, he now has a two inch long indentation on the top left side of his shaved skull and a steel plate beneath the indentation. Since his vocabulary is limited to one word, the word baa, and since he is neither able to eat nor dress nor get out of bed by himself, the ward attendants had to feed, shave, have his bowels move and dress the Captain, as well as satisfy what other wants he might have, all at a proper time just before Williamson arrives in order to prevent a possible breakdown in either his appearance or behavior.

The Captain, apparently upset, utters long and loud baas throughout the preparations. His father, a rancher from Nevada, stands on the right side of the

30

bed attempting to calm him down as the attendants finish. He offers the Captain the urinal, to crank down the bed, to place him in the new electrically propelled wicker wheelchair on the left side of the bed. Each suggestion meets only with louder baas and agitated waves of the Captain's hands. His father is asking him if he wants a hypo when Williamson and the entourage enter the ward.

Immediately the Captain stops baaing.

Williamson, looking neither left nor right, strides rapidly forward. The Captain remains quiet. Williamson reaches the bed. Everyone stops. An aide steps forward and begins reading the citation. Williamson steps up to the Captain, stopping before the wheelchair. He pins a Bronze Star then a Purple Heart over the Captain's left breast pocket. Six flashbulbs explode. He shakes the Captain's hand. The aide finishes reading. Williamson reaches across the bed and shakes hands with the father. Tears appear in the Captain's eyes.

Then Williamson salutes and moves away, the entourage following. The Captain jerks forward, then back, watching them go out along the row of beds. His right hand half-rises to his forehead, then falls, and he begins baaing again, louder and louder, each baa gaining in speed and pitch over the one before.

Surgery

In the doorway through the winter sunlight came
a small four or five year old boy. He was dark headed
with bright eyes and he wore red topped cowboy
boots outside blue levis and a white sweatshirt with
yellow, blue and red triangles and squares on it.
The old woman who ran the store was standing at
the cash register.
My mom sent me, the boy said.
No, she didn't, the old woman said. Her voice came
out in a barely audible rasp, the result of recent
surgery on her thyroid gland. The doctors thought
her thyroid caused the massive tumors she suffered
from. You get up on a stool where I can watch
you, she said.
The breadman, finished with tallying up the
number of units he had just placed on the bread shelf
across the room, looked at the boy and then down at
his figures again.
Mom knows I'm here, the boy said.
You get up there, answered the old woman.
The boy moved to the counter and climbed up on
a stool.

The breadman told the woman how much she owed him and she rang no-sale on the register and paid out the money.

Can I have some ice cream, the boy asked.

No, the old woman said.

Sure, the breadman said, why not. He put a quarter down on the counter.

It's thirty-five, the old woman said.

The breadman took out a dime and two pennies and put them down.

The old woman took the money, put it in the register, then went over to the ice cream tanks.

What's your name, the breadman asked the boy.

The boy was watching the old woman scooping out the ice cream. He didn't respond to the breadman's question.

It's Victor, the old woman said.

The breadman turned around at the sound of the front door being opened. Coming in was a small, young-looking woman, her face flushed from the cold and very pretty, obviously the boy's mother.

Well, mister, she said, you're in for it now, going toward the boy.

He's run off without telling me, she said to the breadman. She looked embarrassed.

The breadman laughed. I bought him the ice cream, he said.

You take the dish home, the old woman said.

Thank you very much. The young woman lifted

the boy off the stool and started to take the ice cream
dish. He wouldn't let her.

Okay, you carry it then, she said.

Thank you again, she said and they went over to
the door then out.

I think the little tiger is in for a whumpin, the
breadman said.

He does that all the time. She's got a new baby and
doesn't keep her eye on him.

He's got that old sweet tooth, you know.

They're jewish, the old woman said.

They have trouble making their kids mind, too,
the breadman said.

Ha, the old woman answered.

Well, the breadman said, I think that should do it,
twenty-six white, fourteen brown.

I hope so.

I left those cakes. It's not too cold out so the kids
should be coming in all weekend.

We'll see, the old woman said.

Okay, see you Tuesday.

The breadman picked up his empty rack off the
floor, put the order pad in his back pocket, then went
out the door. The old woman went back to her stool
against the wall in the corner and started reading
her crossword puzzle book. The radio on the window
ledge next to her was on and she turned the volume up
as a refrigerator kicked on. The program was a talk
show. A woman's voice, talking very fast into a

telephone, was saying mark my words, socialism is
the red carpet to communism, and who is paying for
it, the people that have worked hard all their lives,
that's who, and we're being taxed out of existence
to boot, you mark my words, if something isn't done,
and done fast, within ten years we'll have a communistic,
atheistic existence, believe you me.

The Normal Girl

They married in hometown Minnesota when she
was nineteen. The marriage lasted eight years. During
that time he tried a variety of occupations. He
worked in a gas station. He painted window signs.
He spent three years at college as a painting student
and sold kitchenware door to door. He did layout
for a newspaper, went on unemployment and painted
on his own through one winter and spring. He clerked
in a liquor store. He tended bar. He drove taxicab.
She went where he went, lived where he wanted to
live. Four days after her twenty-sixth birthday, sitting
in their apartment overlooking a swimming pool in
Santa Barbara, California, she told him she wanted
to live a normal life.

"What's that mean?" he said.

"It means I'm a normal girl raised by normal parents
and I want a home and I want a baby."

"Sure you do," he said. "Who doesn't? I do too.
I want a baby by you. I've always wanted a baby
by you."

"No," she said, "that's not what I mean. Don't you
want a child of your own?"

"Not especially."

"Well, I do," she said. "I want us to get a home and you a fulltime job and I want a baby."

"I'd like to have a child."

"And a washing machine. I'm not having a baby unless we have a washing machine."

"I really mean it," she said.

"I believe you. Just don't push and maybe it will happen. I'd like it to happen. I really would."

"I mean it, Douglas."

"And I am thinking of us," she said, "for both of us. Either we make it together or we don't. I want a child."

"I understand," he said.

She left off the conversation and went into the kitchen. She knew not to argue. That only brought rage from him. She would wait and see.

The next day Douglas got up without saying anything, fixed his own breakfast, and left for work without saying goodbye. When he came home in the afternoon he still wasn't talking.

She left him alone.

During dinner he said he had some heavy ideas that needed working out, really strong ideas that would push de Kooning to the wall, maybe, maybe.

He got up from the table, went in the living room, started putting newspaper on the floor. Then he tacked up four huge sheets of clean butcher paper on the wall.

She went in and watched. It was the first painting he had done in some months. He worked fast and athletically, a cigarette in his mouth, attacking the paper in long black smears.

She went to bed and read.

Around midnight he got in bed and wanted to have her.

"No," she said.

"What's the matter."

"Nothing."

"Yes, there is."

"You already know."

"Damn it," he said.

"Just don't touch me."

"You really mean it, don't you."

"Yes."

"Listen, Gwen, consider me in this. I don't know enough yet. I haven't experienced enough yet."

"Having a family isn't dying."

"I don't think so either."

"Then do something, for God's sake."

"That's easy to say."

"You make me sick," she said. "You're so goddamned selfish I can't believe it."

"You're not making sense."

"Oh yes I am. I completely am."

"Listen, hon, listen. Give me one more chance. I've got something going out there. I know it. Really. What I want us to do is move to L.A. That's where

the big art dealers are. It's not New York anymore, it's
L.A. All you have to do is get to know one and doors
open. It's as simple as that."

"Okay," she said. "Go."

"I want us to go."

"No," she said. "This is it. I've moved enough."

"You don't think I can paint."

"No," she answered, "I'm not thinking about you."

"Who the hell is selfish? I mean you've had your
belly filled for the last six years. Where the hell
did that come from?"

"You should go," she said.

"Fuck you," he sprang out of bed. "I will!"

"You know, Douglas, I really mean it."

"So do I!"

She rolled over and turned on the light. He was
standing within arms length, looking straight at her.
She got out on the other side and went to the closet,
reaching up for his suitcase on the top shelf.

"What are you doing?"

She tossed the suitcase on the bed and stood looking
at him, leaning forward, feeling herself losing
control.

"Go!" she said, "go! go! go! you asshole! you
crybaby!"

"I will!" he shouted.

She rushed to the bathroom and slammed the door.

He left about twenty minutes later, apparently
taking most of his things. His big trunk was gone and

all the rolled up papers of new paintings. She imagined
she could hear the car still going away up the street
and she began to feel that something inside her was
really and finally broken and a sick, shaky feeling came
over her. She could hear a car going away. She
walked out of the living room where she had been
standing by the darkened window and returned to
bed. It was totally quiet in the room and she laid face
down, waiting for the feeling to pass.

In the morning when she awoke Douglas wasn't
there. She sat down at the kitchen table and wrote
home, asking her parents what to do. Then she
telephoned home. Come here was her mother's reply;
if he won't take responsibility let him go; there are
plenty of others who will.

"I don't think he's going to return, mama."

"Come home then. I'll send you the money."

"I think I should wait. I don't like the feelings I
have. I do love him."

"Whatever you think is best, darling, but don't
stay alone. Women aren't meant to live alone. You'd be
better off here. If he wants you he can get you here
as well as there. You owe us a visit anyhow. I'll send
you the money. A nice train ride will be good for you."

"Thank you, mama, maybe I will. I want to wait
a while though. I don't want to be impulsive anymore."

"Okay, darling. I'm sending the money this
afternoon."

The money came the next morning, a cashier's check

for four hundred dollars, enough money to pay the rent, buy some new clothes and travel well. She felt momentarily joyful when she saw the amount. It was more money than she had ever seen at one time.

Two days passed without word from Douglas. Gwen spent the time packing her clothes and boxing up their possessions. She didn't expect him to call. She hoped he wouldn't until after she was gone. She wanted him to worry.

When he did call it was what she had expected. He wasn't in L.A., he was in San Francisco, could she come. He was god awful sorry, he wanted her to come, he had located a nice apartment with a view, she would like the city, it was a beautiful city. Her answer was one more week, if he didn't return by then she was going back home to Minnesota, she already had the ticket. He hung up.

The week passed and he didn't return. She took the Santa Fe Chief out of Los Angeles back to Minneapolis but home was a disaster. Once there all the reasons that compelled her to marry years ago returned. Her mother was still patronizing and full of complaints. Her father was distant and unwarm. The town was totally unchanged and dull. Her old girlfriends who had married and stayed were dull and married to boring men. Getting drunk on weekends wasn't her idea of fun. Despite a vow not to, she wrote Douglas and closed by saying she missed him. No reply came and after writing a second letter with the same result she called long distance, hoping he would have a telephone. He did, it was a San Francisco number, when he answered, almost before she knew what she was saying, she blurted out how sorry she was.

"I want to join you," she said.

"I don't have any money," he said. "We'll have to wait."

"I have some. Dad will give us some."

"No," Douglas said, "I don't want any obligations to them."

"You don't want me to come."

"No," he said, "just wait."

"Is there someone else?"

"No, not at all."

"Swear to God?"

"Swear," he said. "Just take it easy. I'll send the money as soon as I can."

"Promise?"

"Promise."

"Okay," she said. "I love you. I know that sounds stupid but I do."

"I love you too."

"Write me."

"I will."

"I can't hang up."

"I know," he said.

But he didn't write for one good reason. He had a new girl, a deeply involving girl. Gwen didn't know this but she knew what he had done in the past and as the days passed without any mail she slowly became frantic and began a series of phone calls usually placed late at night after her parents were asleep. Each time Douglas answered he would deny there was someone else. Gwen would end up crying, telling him she was lonely, desperately lonely. On those occasions when there was no answer she imagined him making love to someone else, fantasies which gradually began to absorb all her attention.

Her mother suggested a psychiatrist and Gwen agreed. The doctor was gentle with her, listened to her story, made no judgments, told her it was not unusual, gave her some tranquilizers, and suggested, if she could, that it might be best to forget Douglas, take what was valuable from the experience, and think of new ways, possibly, to live.

"It's a matter of values," he said. "Douglas is still looking for himself. You're not. May I suggest something further? Start school, for instance? We have a good community college here. You're a very bright girl. You'd do well."

"No," Gwen said, "I hate it here. I never really understood that but it's true. I don't belong in this life."

"What do you mean?"

"I belong somewhere else. Out on the coast. If not with Douglas at least with someone like him. Not entirely like him. Someone grown up but someone who isn't boring, who isn't dead inside. Sometimes I'm afraid I'm becoming dead inside and I get scared, really scared."

"I see," the doctor said.

At home Gwen told her parents she wanted to return to the coast, to go to San Francisco. Surprisingly, her father gave her a hug, told her he had always liked Douglas and wrote her out a check for two hundred dollars.

"My blessing, sweetheart," he said.

Later that day when her father had left the house her mother tried to talk her out of it but Gwen wouldn't listen.

Four days later she arrived in San Francisco and checked into the Y.W.C.A. For a moment, standing in the lobby, she debated whether to call first or to freshen up and pay a surprise visit. A slight edge of fear decided her to call.

Douglas was home. She said she hadn't meant to startle him, wasn't trying to spy on him, yes, she was in the city. She hoped he wanted to see her, she had changed, she was willing to live on his terms, willing to live free, she would even work while he painted, she did believe in his work, was he painting? could she come to wherever he was?

"As a matter of fact," he said, "I was just going downtown when you called. I'll be right down; say twenty minutes."

"Oh, good," she said.

44

"But I better warn you," he said. "I don't want you to misunderstand. I've already filed for a divorce."

"No," she said.

"I'm sorry, Gwen, it's true. The papers have already been sent out to you."

"What's that mean?"

"It means I want a divorce."

"No!"

"I'm sorry but it's true."

"You don't mean it."

"I do."

"My God," she said.

"Listen," he said, "be calm. I'm really glad you're here. Really. Now don't go away. I'll be right down. I really do want to talk to you."

She listened to him hang up the phone and she held on to the receiver. She waited for the buzzing to stop and then realized she was crying, her mouth actually fluttering. She pulled open the door and went out, not hanging up the phone. She went back and hung it up. She walked over to a couch by the far wall and sat down.

"That son of a bitch," she thought, "he's not going to do this to me. He can't. I won't let him."

She got up and walked over to the ladies room. Going inside she caught a glimpse of herself crying in the long mirror above the washbasins. She watched the door shut behind her, then bent over, washed her hands, then her face, taking off all the makeup. She looked at herself carefully, then took out a small plastic bottle of Murine and rinsed out her eyes. Her face was puffy and red and she ran the cold water tap and splashed the water on her cheeks. Then she took a paper towel, soaked it, pressed it across her eyes. After a minute her stomach stopped jumping and she looked at herself. She took out mascara and did her eyes. She penciled on fresh eyebrows and put on a pale shade of lipstick.

She looked good. Her face was still tan from living in Santa Barbara and her blue eyes looked bright within the shadowed lashes. Her cheeks had color because of the crying. She laughed and took out her hairbrush. Stroking her hair calmed her like it always did.

She was sitting on a yellow couch by the big windows in the side lobby when Douglas came in. She was leafing through a magazine and as he approached he noticed her hair was longer, fuller looking, and her face looked good, beautiful, happy.

Confused, he gave her a kiss, sat down hard on the couch, said he had only a few minutes to stay.

"Well," she said, "I guess I certainly have made a mess of things, haven't I."

"We both have."

"It's not too late, is it? I mean I really have changed. Back home I realized that I don't want to live my parents' life. I couldn't stand it there. I suppose you have contempt for me."

"No."

"I want to stay here. You were right; it is a lovely city. If things don't work out I'm prepared to stay and get a job. I mean you can see me whenever you want but I'll get a place of my own and stay out of your affairs."

"You can stay if you want," he said. "That's your right but I don't think it would be fair to see you."

"Don't you love me?"

He sat for a moment.

"Yes," he said finally, "but I don't want to see you."

"That doesn't make sense."

"That's all I can say."

"There's someone else."

"No," he said, "there isn't. It isn't that simple."

She persisted for a moment, then stopped, suddenly thinking of all the mistakes she had made, the time she had slashed his paintings, her frigidity.

He said he thought the best thing to do was put her on the train again and send her back home.

"I'm sorry, Gwen, I am. I don't want to be cruel but I'm sorry."

They sat in silence and then she agreed, saying she had just enough money for train fare. He took out his wallet and gave her forty dollars.

"I don't need it," she said.

"Take it."

"I have enough money. I just wanted to see . . ."

"To see what?"

"Nothing," she said, feeling tears just beginning to start up behind her voice. "Would you have someone go upstairs and get my suitcase. Nothing is unpacked. Both my coat and the suitcase are lying on the bed."

"Don't you want to stay over one night, to rest up?"

"No. I'd like to leave now."

He stood up, asking what her room number was. She told him. He walked away toward the desk. She stood up, smoothed her skirt, then walked fast to the ladies room. She felt dizzy and inside she pushed open a toilet door and threw up into the bowl. She wiped her mouth with some paper then threw up again. The odor of her vomit assaulted her and other odors and she stood up, feeling better, yet drained, somehow outside her own body. She went to the door without washing her face. Douglas wasn't in the lobby. She went back in, crying again. There was stuff on her blouse that she scraped at. It wouldn't come out. She drenched it in water and tried to stop crying. She tore her blouse, going wild for a moment.

"That filthy bastard," she said, "that filthy rotten bastard."

Gradually she calmed down, her mind going quiet, then clear. She stared at her face in the mirror.

"You're not a bad looking girl," she said, "you're not at all."

She felt a charge of tension everywhere around her but not inside. She felt quiet inside. She brushed back her hair with her hand and then went out.

Douglas was standing by the couch, her coat draped over his arm. Her suitcase rested on the floor.

"I've called the airport," he said. "I've made reservations on a ten o'clock flight. Let's go out to dinner and maybe a movie."

"A movie," she said.

"Something," he said, "or walk around."

She took the coat from him, looking at his face, somehow looking at exactly what his face presented, capturing not his gestures or how he seemed to be, but exactly those few lines coming out from the corners of his eyes, lines she had never seen before, age lines, he had actually aged, she had never noticed it before.

"No," she said, "nothing. I don't think I'd like to wait. I'd like to catch the train."

"Are you sure?"

"Yes," she said.

"Are you all right?"

"Yes," she said. "You go on."

"I'm sorry," he said.

"So am I," she said.

"Does the train leave this afternoon? I mean is there one?"

"It doesn't matter," she answered. "Please go."

He Won't Hurt You

He didn't want us to dislike him. He wanted us to
think him the most wonderful fellow who ever lived.
And so he was. He stood in the living room, talking
fast, wearing his work clothes, sunlight covering his
left side. A nigger was killed in the rain, crushed
beneath a boxcar. It was a nigger but the skin was
white. The rain had washed it clean. And so we laughed
at this point, laughed at his pantomimed eyes wide
in terror. An old couple stalled their car at a crossing.
The old woman was too terrified to move. The old
man went around to pull her out. Just then the train
hit. Just like a football the old man took off fifty
feet in the air. More grinning, of course, and laughter.
He shifted back away from us, still talking, more of
his face coming into the light, standing back by the
plants, avoiding the dog asleep on the rug. He tipped
to the side, head up, petted the dog. Everything was
scattered for hundreds of feet. Coroners carry long
black bags made of rubber to chuck the parts into.
They found the old woman's cunt. Had hold of it by
the shorthairs, he said, the shorthairs. The coroner
had to chuck it into the bag. His eyes were bright,

alive, blond wings of hair stood out over his ears. He spun around, then shot us with a finger, bam, bam, bam. Railroadin, he said, that's the kind of stories they tell me.

Three

Country Wedding in the City

Then she walked over to the groom.
"You fuck you shit you piss ass stink! Blow my hole!"
"Weow!" said he, "are you ever primed!"
"Good luck, George," friends called out.
Did they all live in the country?
Nope.
Only Dave, the best man. Dave owned a Peugeot.
That afternoon he got in the back, shot up 500 mgs
of paraboxelynic, flew out the window and slowly
rose up over the city into the country fair air of the
sky.
    "Whatcha doing up there, Dave?" friends cried out.
Smilin, Dave waved.

Seize the Time

John, an active university revolutionary, learned
Steven's ideas of the world were different than his.
Since John liked Steven's style, his name, his ability
to hustle chicks, he set out to educate Steven in
revolutionary cause and rhetoric. Steven, he felt,
would look good on the barricades.

Steven, however, resisted, insisting against John's
personality. Yet he found himself naturally curious
about a world view of which he self-admittedly knew
little. And so, after a normal length of time resisting,
Steven finally said, "Okay, I'll go to the next meeting
of the collective. I've nothing to lose. If there I see
that what you believe helps man to become a better
man, I'll accept your arguments and join the
movement."

John, however, when he heard this, far from being
delighted, was deeply depressed, saying to himself,
"If Steven goes to a meeting, sees the inexperience on
the faces of the kids, fails to see the humor in the
almost inane repetition of all the raps going down, he'll
end up thinking all revolutionary ideas are frauds."

Turning to Steven, he said, "No, man; it's not a

good idea. Just listen to me, read what I have to give you, then think on it."

"No," Steven answered, "I want to see for myself."

A few nights later Steven sat in on a meeting. At first, listening to the dialogues, he formed no opinions. But after a time he began to see the aura of romance about the revolutionaries: the boldest speakers had the best-looking girls. And, as he listened, he formed the conclusion that, without exception, the better speakers were completely certain their viewpoints were right, were morally correct, that contrary to what they were asking for — justice — they condemned all men not on their side as traitors to mankind.

Steven was unhappy with what he saw. He left the meeting quietly, holding his complaints for an encounter with John.

They met the next day.

John, quickly scanning Steven's face, had not the slightest hope of his conversion. They had coffee together and talked of academic affairs, both avoiding any discussion of the movement. Finally, though, John could stand it no longer.

"So," he asked, "what happened at the meeting?"

"Well," Steven said, "what I saw was a bunch of guys romantically in love with themselves, and, far from being involved in dreams that would make them better human beings, I only saw the same old shit: cats looking to be admired by their peer group."

"I thought that would happen," John said.

"But," Steven continued, "what struck my imagination was that while the radicals were responding to new ideas in old human ways, it was obvious that the ideas they were trying to express were true and good, ideas that would hasten the end of a competitive society, notions of racial superiority, sound the death knell of the ideas of heroes, leaders, supermen; ideas that would change this world for the good and joy of all if enough people understood them.

"In short, by participating I was converted and freed."

"Wow," John said, smiling. He was suddenly the happiest of men. The revolution was working. Rushing Steven up from his seat, he took him across the street to the Id Bookstore and bought him a copy of Mao's thoughts.

When other revolutionaries heard of Steven's conversion they quickly became friends, solid friends. And right now, at almost any time of the day, you can go up on the Avenue in the U district and see Steven standing on the street, a red Mao button in his lapel, waiting for the revolution to come.

Stiff

Charley Winterbourne drinks muscatel up on the
third floor. Like they say, he says, Goodnight, Chet,
Goodnight, David, and Walter, Walter Cronkite
when he says that's the way it was, Walter, Charley
says. Charley sits stocking footed on the edge of
the bed. He pours more wine into his glass. The wine
pours gold and brown and clear. Walter, Walter
Cronkite. Charley lifts his glass. No one else is in
the room. Out the window the lights of San Francisco
are yellow. The sky is a soft dark blue. Goodnight,
folks, goodnight, that's the way it was. Charley still
has his hat on. His grin is sleepy and he is sleepy too.
Goodnight, Chet, Goodnight, David, and Walter,
Walter Cronkite when he says Goodnight, folks,
goodnight.

Street

He was peddling speed and coke, a very flashy
dealer in tapestry bellbottoms, yellow ruffled shirt,
leather coat, leather headband, long hair flowing down
to his shoulders. We walked together for a minute
going up past City Lights Bookstore.

"Naw, that's bullshit, man, cause I've been hassled
with too much, I'm not going to be hassled with again.
If they come they'd better come in pairs cause one
isn't going to do it and if he shoots he'd better kill
me cause I'll shoot the fucker if he misses and if he
kills me then I'm free cause when you're dead you're
free."

Then: "I want to be free and we can't be free as
long as one of those pigs is alive."

Then: "No narc would come up here, man, cause
if they did they'd be killed with fucking butcher
knives."

Another cat with long hair and narrow stovepipe
bells was standing at the corner waiting for the light.
He overheard us.

"With machine guns, man," this guy said, "every
fucking one of them."

Kid Colt Outlaw in Wyoming

The ghosts of a hundred Pawnee warriors glared
eerily from the ancient indian burial grounds. Kid Colt,
senses alert, the sound of motion whipping his head,
was advancing into a phantom ambush, the oilblack
rain sky alive with the possibility of psychic death.
Suddenly the Kid's mind flashed back to the strange
events which had led to this fateful encounter.
Lightning bolted through the window onto the Kid's
crib bars, dancing about, then shot into a light socket,
leaving the Kid peacefully sleeping, the room empty
of fury, while outside it rained, inside the Kid's parents
in shock had looked on, helpless to rescue the baby,
it all took place so fast, and there was no need, strange
child! A mystery to be unfolded! At eleven strange
currents said ask God to strike you dead, ask, at
nineteen philosophy 101 some girl had stood up saying
who am I so everyone laughed, everyone except the
Kid then spreading his hands out into the inscrutable
while now, now, high beyond the clouds the unseen
moon rose orangely over the earth thus the evening
found Kid Colt taking it all back home, hurtling
through deja-vu, bam! what was that? ghosts, the Kid

thought, looking back, don't make noise. Something
there was melting into the shadows. Wind was howling
over the mesa. Then it happened! the Yamaha seized
up! the back tire skidding out, screaming, he slid!
Quick as a flash the Kid kicked it out of gear, controlled
the slide, popping the clutch, headlight flaring
dimly in the rain. He stopped and stomped. It wouldn't
kick over. He tried again. Voices floated to him: Kid,
Kid, the spirits of the Pawnee were with you tonight,
white brother, we saw you fight with the weapons of
warriors long dead, all are grateful. The Kid
dismounted, pushing up his visor, his breath fogging
the air. He started rolling the bike off into the brush,
the search for America breaking down, his real
journey about to commence. Desperately, he longed
for a Standard Station.

Sather Gate

She was a non-student, a runaway from smalltown
lowclass oklahoma, she said, come to Berkeley she
didn't know why, her boyfriend was into an off-the-wall
movie trip, like we were into this thing where the
camera is your brother so you're free to do anything,
do any thing, every thing you can think of, a sex
thing, everyone was up on acid, and I began thinking,
shit, man, we're into this thing where all learning is
considered good, like that brought us the hydrogen
bomb, you know.

Later, leaving her apartment, that's the real
problem, she said, it's too damn bad everything has
to be so casual.

Four

Early Morning Wind

In a terrible snowstorm when John was a boy they
had brought a donkey steam-engine up that road and
down into the creekbed, the hollar. John told that
at the supper table, eating panfried chicken, beans,
green salad. John's farm was clean. Sarah had never
seen the ocean. She asked Lee to send her some
shells from the ocean, seashells. John said, Well, we'll
go see the old place in the morning.

They rode on John's tractor out along a high bank
on a tilt along a long, high-staked turkeyfence, the
turkeys all running hard and banging into each other
when John crashed the horn. They agitate me so I
agitate them, he said.

It was a bright morning with the sky blue and
the footgrass dry and dusty. The road disappeared
as they came to what looked like a small farmhouse.
Woods started in back of the house and went away
as far as you could see in a covering of endless hills.
John stopped the tractor and got off. A man came
out of the house and to the fence.

"Morning," John said. "This here's my cousin's
grandson from out west. I'd like to take him back into
the hollar and show him where the old place was."

"Sure enough, John." the man said. He unlocked the padlock on the aluminium gate and let them through.

The road broke immediately into some trees, the tractor jouncing and shaking. Lee tried to imagine running a horse through. His grandfather had worn a diamond ring on his little finger and had a racing horse, the baby of the family, the only one to go to school, too. As they went on Lee got John to talk about him. They didn't call him that, John said, they called him Faye, he was sure enough a rounder, one thing I recall was when he'd got himself and his guitar up in one of them limestone caves up near the ridge and started hooing in there at the boys out working in the corn around the bend — when they heard that sound they just took off, wasn't till the afternoon that your great granddad rounded them up and when he found out it was Faye that had done it he gave him a solid whippin — a rounder, for sure that was him . . .

The rest of the trip continued rough, yet beautiful, they followed a barely discernible road, more a track, along the hillsides, often driving around huge boulders and fallen trees, and then they turned down and were in a draw where they went along a dry creekbed that wound around between wooded cliffs. John told him it might be hard to believe but that back in the nineties and during the turn of the century a lot of folks lived on those hillsides, farming down here in the bottom, hundreds of folks. It was hard to believe. The slopes were straight up and down in places, entirely covered with growth of all kinds. There were no houses nor did it look like there ever could have been.

After a time the creekbed opened into a near valley, about a hundred yards wide. John stopped the tractor and shut it off. The sound of thousands of cicadas droned off the hills. They walked across the dry rounded stones of the creekbed and went over to the slope. Lee had lost all sense of direction. It was extremely hot. John pointed left high along the hillside.

"The big house was up there," he said. "That was the second house, the one I remember as a boy."

"Where was the first?"

"Right where you're standing," John said.

He showed Lee the outlines of the foundation, actual squarecut blocks of limestone brought from Rogers forty miles away. The blocks were still in the ground, dirted over. Lee cleaned one off with the toe of his boot.

"Three kids in this house, the other eight up there," John said.

That was all there was to it. They walked up to where the cornfields had been and then came back to the tractor.

The next day John and Sarah took Lee into Claymore and then down to Rogers to see a man named Harnish. He'd been a pal of Faye's and was now in the V.A. Hospital. John said maybe he could tell him more about the old days.

The V.A. Hospital was new looking, recently constructed. The lawns looked old, though, and rich. They went inside and down a broad corridor. Harnish was in the end ward. The room was pleasant and sunny. Harnish was sitting up in his bed, two white pillows behind his back. Lee expected an old looking man and was surprised. Harnish's face was lean and tan and his hair was dark with only flecks of grey in it.

"Bill," John said.

"Hello, John."

"Bill, this here is Lee Hatcher, Faye Hatcher's boy's boy. You remember Faye?"

"Sure," Harnish said, "I do." He was silent for a moment, then he said, "It's bad, John, they've got to operate."

"Well," John said, "they'll do all right."

"No, John, they won't. "

"Sure they will."

"No, it's terminal, John."

"I don't believe that, Bill," Sarah said.

"Don't tell Judy now. She doesn't know."

"Hasn't she been here?"

"No, I haven't let her."

On the way back John pulled in to a Dairy Queen Drive-In and bought them all double-decker ice cream cones. Sarah told Lee a nice story about Bill and Faye that she had heard of and then one about her grown kids and how Laurie, who would be Lee's cousin twice removed, had learned how babies were made and had him and herself laughing.

That evening after supper John asked Lee to come outside with him and he'd show him the main barn, the only thing they hadn't gotten around to doing. John was a large man, nearly six three and easily two hundred and thirty pounds. He'd worn big-mac overalls, a blue work shirt and a felt hat all four days Lee stayed there, even on the visit to the hospital. He was dressed this way now and Lee studied him as they walked out across the lawn and then into the barnyard. John was dark like Granddad Hatcher had been, all the Hatchers had indian blood in them.

They went inside the barn and John walked over to a stall, then turned around.

"Well, Lee," he said, "it's been real nice havin you stay with us."

"Thank you John, I've learned a lot."

"Tell me one thing, Lee. It's something I've been meaning to ask you. You don't have the true faith do you?"

"No, sir," Lee said, "you mean the Baptist, don't you?"

"Yes sir, I do."

"No, not right now," Lee answered.

"Have you any faith?"

"No sir, I guess I don't."

"You think about it, son. It would make this old

71

man mighty happy to think that someday you would."

"All right, John," Lee said, "I will think about it."

"It would make me mighty happy," John said.

"I'll try my best, John."

Becky: West Florida Romance

"That's them," Reeves said.

Down the highway under the trees some people stood by a white mailbox. The little girl was standing behind the woman. A boy in a teeshirt stood next to the girl. They both looked small, babies, really.

I looked at Reeves. His alcoholic's face was up over the wheel with his eyes squinted, trying to see through the dirty windshield and glare off the highway. Fine veins branched redly under his cheeks. He was excited for sure.

We went off the road and along the shoulder.

"Becca'll ride up here with us," he said. "You'll see what I mean."

We came alongside and he stopped the car.

"Well," he said out my window, "I made it after all."

"I knew you would," the woman said. "I wasn't worried."

"That's good," Reeves said.

The woman smiled at me and pulled the children forward. Her hair was bleached, the roots showing dark. Her eyebrows were painted on, like those I had seen in photographs of mexican whores in boxes outside Mexico City around the turn of the century.

"Com'on, Paul," she said, tugging at the boy. He resisted, apparently scared of me. His face was dirty and he wore thick spectacles, his eyes large and milky blue behind the glass. The woman pushed him forward, then the little girl.

"This here's a Washington boy," Reeves said. Picked him up outside Lassiter."

"Pleased to meet you," the woman said. She pushed the boy again and I reached over and opened the back door.

Reeves leaned over the seat and as the little girl got in he lifted her up over and stood her between us.

The woman then the boy got in and I closed their door.

"This sure is good of you, Pat," the woman said.

"How's my ol Becca?" Reeves said. He had his arm around the child's waist. "Can you give your ol uncle Pat a kiss? Hmmm? Can you?"

The girl was looking at me, her head slightly above mine, her eyes clear child's eyes. She was a beautiful little girl.

Reeves put his hand on her leg.

I shook my head at her.

"The bank closes at three, don't it?" the woman asked.

Reeves pulled Becca to him. She put her arm around his neck.

"Ain't she somethin," he said.

Becca gave him a kiss. Reeves moved his hand up under her dress. She kissed again and started to bounce

74

up and down on the seat, the cushion gently moving beneath me.

"Well, Pat," I said, "I believe you. I think I'll get out here if you don't mind. I'd like to walk for a bit."

"Out here?" Reeves said, looking over Becca's shoulder. He had a perplexed look on his face.

"Right," I said. I opened the door and got out. In back the woman was looking in her purse. She looked up startled.

"Sure," Reeves said. He reached around Becca and closed the door.

I stepped back.

Becca didn't look, watching Reeves as he took the wheel. Then the car moved off, bouncing as it hit the pavement, sun flashing sharply off its dusty flanks. The boy's face appeared at the rear window, soon vanishing into shadow.

I watched them for a moment and then turned around and walked over to the mailbox.

Leona Pride, it read. 'A widow woman,' Reeves had said. 'Yes sir, really honest to God in love, the both of us. No, she don't know. She thinks it's her I'm interested in.'

War Songs

I've been thinking of you and hope you have a
Happy Birthday tomorrow. Hope the day is correct. I
told Gloria how we used to have mental telepathy in
Spokane, ha. ha.

Hope Jay is well and I have wondered if you got
over the ulcer trouble. Hope Dave is well and happy.
Do they have children? Excuse the mistakes. My
glasses need changing as I don't see too good. I
remember Martha's daughter Lynn and what caused
her to die so young? That must have been very hard
on Martha and family.

Mother and Melissa have been fine. Fred is about
the same (bedridden), he is up a little each day. I
told you about his broken neck and he never walked
again. Donna gets pretty tired from the care. She
had to train about like a nurse to care for him. Rena
Jean lives in Tacoma. She has two girls. Diane lives
at Skyway has two boys and one girl. Betty and Lora
had some nerve trouble. Betty is fine but Lora isn't
too well yet. Think Tom is a lot to blame. David (their
boy) just twenty-one eloped with a Japanese girl
and the dad and other grandma disowned him. Lora

and Tom bought a new model home at Bothell and
Tom won't let him bring her there at all. The rest of us
will be kind to her if that's what he wants. Lora
is a Christian and will be good to her. I don't approve
of mixed marriages but will always be good to her.
He met her at the University of Wash.

I was very sad about the middle of November.
John's brother Ralph had a heart attack. He lived
just a few days and passed away. We got two cute
cards to send him at the Veteran's Hospital in Walla
Walla and had some pictures for him too but he
died before I got them there. He was still Catholic so
they had a rosary and mass. I couldn't go as I was low
on money. He was like a brother to me all these
years. He was up to Davenport in August and helped
Walter do some painting. He got diabetes and I
know that he had been doctoring. Walter and Helen
and families went to Walla Walla for the funeral. On
the way home they got about twenty miles from Walla
Walla and Walter had a heart attack at the wheel.
Mike took over (he is eighteen now) and they took
him to the hospital. He didn't have any heart damage.
The electric card-o-graph showed the old arteries
ruptured and the new ones took over. I told you he
had heart surgery a year ago, I believe. Had he not had
the operation he would have died on the spot. We
had two heart attacks within two weeks in the
family and you can imagine how upset I was — after
going through it with John. The Walla Walla heart

doctors who did the surgery seem to think he is
getting along o.k. Doris (John's sister) isn't very well
her blood pressure went high and she had chest pains
from the strain of it all. Wish I could go visit them.
I haven't been to Walla Walla for six years or
Davenport.

Guess you will think this is some letter with all
the bad news. I am just getting over a virus. It
started in my stomach and then I got a sore throat
I lost my voice and it hit my lungs and I nearly had
pneumonia for a week or two. I have been several
weeks getting over the bronchial cough and cold.
I had been planning to write for several weeks. I felt
pretty bum.

Donald took Gloria on a long trip in August she
was gone all month. She was in Wash., Idaho, Montana,
Yellowstone, S. Dakota, Nebraska, Kansas, Missouri,
Arkansas, Tennessee (saw Elvis Presley's home in
Memphis), New Orleans, Texas, Dallas, New Mexico
(saw the Carlsbad Caverns), Nevada, Las Vegas,
Reno, Northern Calif., Ore., and home. They stayed
at motels with pools and T.V. and she had the time
of her life. We sure missed her though. She and
Julie both had the mumps this summer.

Do you ever hear from any of the Bureau of
Reclamation people or from the Corps of Engineers?

Think of some often. Heard "If I Loved You" and "Stranger in Paradise" yesterday, war songs. Thought of Mitch. I have never got over that.

Wish you could come over sometime would love to see you. Don't think I thanked you for the lovely fruit cake. It sure was nice to have and I use the tin for a cookie jar.

Love,

Klamath Falls

Mark stood up and held out his hand. The car was a pickup, dull red with a camper on the back. An old man was driving, no one else with him. Bill sat and watched. Mark was waving his arm up and down. The pickup went past, then slowed, the red brake lights flashing off, on.

"Let's go, man," Mark said, grabbing his pack. He started running.

Bill got up, taking his pack through one of the loops. He ran halfway, then slowed to a walk. Nosed over on the shoulder, the pickup was running, its tailend sticking out on the highway. Mark was at the cab and opening the door.

"Morning," Bill heard Mark say. "How far you going?"

"Morning," came the answer.

Bill walked up behind Mark. The driver looked at him.

"Where you boys going?"

"K. Falls," Mark said.

"Both of you?"

"Right," Mark said.

"Well, that's just fine. Hop on in."

"You going up there?" Bill said.

"Up near there."

"Great," Mark said. He stepped on the running board and swung in, sliding across the seat.

"Com'on, man," he said to Bill.

Bill climbed up and got in, keeping his pack on his lap. He closed the door.

"All set?" asked the driver.

"Yep," Mark answered.

"Good. Here we go."

He let out the clutch and the pickup lurched ahead, starting for the ditch, then cutting sharply for the highway.

"Man," Bill said.

"Been waiting long?" asked the driver.

"All night," said Mark. "We're going back to school. We've been out on spring vacation."

"Is that so," the driver said. "My name's Billy, Billy Wetzel."

"Mark," Mark said, "and that's Bill."

"Pleased to meet you. It's a privilege to meet such nice looking boys."

Bill looked at him. Underneath that blue baseball cap he was fruity looking, all right, weak, his mouth crumpled in without any teeth.

"Thank you," Mark said.

Bill said nothing. He took off his coat, wadded it up, put it against the window. He slumped over against it and closed his eyes, listening to the sound of the engine pulling them steadily on.

"You boys ever do any posing?" It was the old man's voice.

"Posing?" Mark asked. "You mean modeling?"

"No," said the old man, "posing."

"Artists?"

"No; people."

"How's that?"

"Tables, you see, you walk . . ."

"Tables," Mark laughed, "you mean walk around with no clothes on . . ."

"That's it."

". . . in front of a bunch of people?"

"That's it."

"Ha," Mark laughed. "How about you, Bill?"

"Shit," Bill said. He closed his eyes again. He knew it. He knew it all along. He could tell by the way the pickup had approached.

Mark laughed again.

"It ain't so hard," the old man said. "Pays good money, too."

"Tell me about it," Mark said. "I mean what do you do?"

"You walk around on these tables . . ."

"Who's there? I mean is it just men or women or what?"

"Everybody. All kinds of people."

"Shoot," Mark laughed. "Don't you feel kind

of funny?"

"Oh, no," the old man said. "Why should you? They pay you. It's just work."

"Yeah, but I mean, well, what do they do? Just look at you?"

"Some of them."

"Jesus," Bill said, "that's sick."

"Why, hell," the old man said, "I've even had guys pay me ten dollars just so's they could kiss my belly. You ever had your belly kissed?"

He was looking at Bill.

"Fuck, no," Bill said, "and I'd kill any son of a bitch that tried."

Mark laughed.

The old man looked away. Bill stared at him, then sat back. He expected Mark to say something. Mark would. Mark would say or do anything.

"You know, son," the old man said, "you're a lucky boy."

"Why?" Mark asked.

"No, not you. The other fellow."

"How's that?" Bill sat up. The old man was looking out at the road, both hands on the steering wheel.

"You've got a lovely set of teeth, sir . . ."

"Ha," Mark laughed.

". . . a blessing, you bet your life it is."

Bill looked at him, then sat back again, closing his eyes.

"Why is that?" Mark said.

"No taste," said the old man. "You can't taste a damn thing."

"Is that right," Mark said.

"That's true," the old man said. "Makes you like a little baby again."

"I see," Mark said.

"Can't eat anything solid."

Mark didn't answer that and the voices stopped. There wasn't any talking for some time. Bill felt himself almost go asleep. He opened his eyes. They were going up a long, slow grade with huge pines lining the sides. Up ahead pools of light formed mirages on the blacktop.

"Yes, sir," the old man said, "pretty country up here."

"It is," Mark agreed.

"I always enjoy it. I come up here all the time."

"Where you from?"

"Mission Beach, down in San Diego."

"That's a long way," Mark said.

"I'm always on the road one time or another."

"You pick up many hitchhikers?"

"Always do," the old man said. "Last summer I picked up a fellow from Harvard. Spent six weeks together."

"No kidding," Mark said.

"Nice fellow. Just graduated. Went all the way to Canada with me. You ever been up there? Most of it's still virgin country, you know."

"That's what I understand," Mark said.

"You boys drink beer?"

They crested the grade and started around a curve. The right front wheel went off the pavement.

"Jesus," Bill said.

The old man let off the gas and slowed the truck. The curve fed into another and then they were going down a long sloping straight and then onto a long, white looking concrete bridge. Far below was a creek, browngreen between its banks.

"Sure," Mark said. "That's really pretty down there."

"It is," the old man answered. "Not good for much, though. Too many people use it."

"Yeah, I suppose," Mark said.

"You've got to pack back into the mountains to get real country."

"I guess that's so," said Mark. "I'd like to do that. So would Bill."

"By myself," Bill said.

"What?"

"By myself," Bill repeated.

"Hey," Mark said. "I thought you were asleep. Sorry, man."

"No," Bill said.

"You boys got sleeping bags? You'd need sleeping bags to do that."

"No, not this trip," Mark said. "We've been visiting friends down in Berkeley. We didn't expect to have to sleep out."

"Couldn't go back in the mountains without good bags."

They went along another curve, the road well shadowed by the trees, only a narrow swath of blue sky over them.

"You boys ever been to San Francisco?"

"Sure," Mark said. "How about it, Bill?"

"Ever go in the bars there?"

"We're not old enough to drink," Bill said.

"There's one place there you should see," the old man said, "just one big room."

"What for?" Mark asked.

"Couples," the old man said, "ten couples every night. All's they have in there is one light and a rug, a nice thick rug, nothing else . . ."

"Nothing else?"

". . . just one tiny light on way down at the end and a few cushions. No chairs, no tables, nothing . . ."

"Wow," Mark said, "what happens?"

"You name it."

"You mean balling?"

"Everything," the old man said, "sucking, fucking, switching . . ."

"I see," Mark said.

"Doors open at ten and stay open till there's ten couples then they close till six in the morning. No one can get in or get out until six."

"What's it cost?"

"Ten bucks a person."

"Two hundred dollars a night," Mark said.

"Every night," said the old man.

"That's a lot of dough."

"It's a lot of fun."

"I bet," Mark said. "I bet it is."

"You boys have to stop?"

Bill looked away from him. Coming toward them on the right was a clearing in the trees and a service station.

"Not me," Bill said.

"Sure," Mark said. "I could stand to wash up."

"I've got to," said the old man. He pumped the brakes and turned the wheel. They went off the highway into the station lot. He stopped at the side of the building.

"Coming?" He shut off the engine.

"Right," Mark answered.

The old man opened his door and got out. As he walked around the front of the truck he looked in at them. He was a lot bigger than Bill had thought he was. From a distance he didn't look so old. Bill watched him go over to the men's room.

"Well?" Mark said.

"Fuck you," Bill said. He opened his door.

"What the hell's wrong?"

"You figure it out," Bill said.

"Okay, man, that's all right with me."

"Okay." Bill lifted his pack and stepped down.

"I kind of feel sorry for the old coot, you know."

"Well, you know what to do." Bill put on his pack.

"What does that mean?"

"Go on in there."

"Where?"

"In the head, man, in the head."

"Look, Bill . . ."

"Look, nothing, Mark. All you have to do is split
for the head. That'll cinch it for you. He'll take you to
the moon."

"You're really an asshole, Bill, you know that?"

"Me!" Bill said. "Ha!"

"I said I was sorry, man. I am. It was a mistake."

Bill looked at him.

"You know, man," said Mark, "you don't know shit.
You don't know the first goddamn thing about people."

"I'm learning pretty fast," Bill said. "I know that."

"You've got a lot more to learn, man."

"We'll see," Bill said. "We'll fucking see."

"Okay, take off."

"I am, man."

"All right," Mark said.

Bill walked back along the side of the pickup and
then out toward the road. There weren't any cars
coming. The highway was empty. He hoped one would
come soon. He didn't want to be standing waiting
when Billy and Mark went by. What a rotten trip
this had been. It really had.

"But not me," Bill said fiercely. "Not me."

88

The Big Apple

Their first time in Manhattan they stayed with
Felicia's college roommate, Dolores, and her roommate,
a good-looking boy named Gary.

The second night there, Gary, who had been gone
all evening, came back to the flat with a man named
Morton. Morton was about thirty-five and wore a
grey suit. Dolores was away visiting an aunt and uncle
somewhere up on Long Island and Gary and Morton
slept together in Dolores' bed. David lay awake
listening to them.

It makes me sick, he said.

Ssh, Felicia said. Live and let live, Babe.

Not me, David said, I'm getting the fuck out of
here. I hate this goddamn place.

Felicia reached out and held on.

Come back here, you silly, she said.

She kissed his arm and pulled him back down.
Listen, she said, you know that I know Gary from
school, don't you? Do you know that?

No, David said.

Well, I do, Felicia said. And I worry about him. I
used to worry about him a lot. He's had some pretty

horrible things happen to him. His mother slept with
him until he was sixteen. Did I tell you I slept with
him once? I think I'm the only girl he's ever slept with.

No, David said, you didn't tell me. Did it make
any difference. He seems pretty happy the way he is.

Not like us, she said, now here, come here, let's
be happy too.

Rides

It was dark before another car stopped. The driver,
a large man in his forties, asked Jackson to sit up
front. He talked a lot about his mother and then about
Jesus. He said Jesus knew things that no one else knew.
At Chesapeake Bay they had to wait for the ferry.
The ferry arrived and they drove down into the hold.
Jackson got out and went up the steel stairway. The
driver followed him. "Forgive me," he said, "you must
forgive me." He touched Jackson's arm. "I pray and
pray." He stopped in the lounge. Jackson went outside
along the railings. The wind blowing out of the dark
was sharp and cold. Across the deck yellow lights
outlined the bow. Later that night, sleeping off the
road, Jackson dreamed. He dreamed he was floating
inside a river, drifting on his back. Overhead, far
up on the surface, poisonous snakes lashed upstream,
their bellies a strange cold green.

Five

Army

Carol Ann came in, mildly ripped, happy in her
eyes. Where is that boy, she said, ough, god damn him,
I'm going to eat that boy up when he gets here,
love, yes I love him, I love everybody, people are
everything, aren't they, what else is there, sex, what
else have I got going for me besides my body, drugs,
she laughed, her eyes full of secrets, old age, no, I'm
not afraid of old age, everybody gets old, what do
you expect, no, the only thing I'm afraid of is
obsolescence, I'm afraid of getting obsolete, no one
has to do that, no one, now repeat after me, women
know more than men, repeat, women know more than
men. We laughed together, she went out the door into
the street.

Lucy in the Sky

Standing up, head tipped forward, listening (Gray,
a twenty-three year old college graduate surfing until
he is drafted, not to the Vietnamese war, yet he
would like to see a war. Blond, moderately long hair,
tan, levis, sky blue boat deck shoes, striped red and
white surf shirt), mind jammed with the sensory
impressions of this house: its colored crystal prisms
strung by wire across the windows, its psychedelic rock
music posters on the walls, the mauve and rose and
cream scarves partitioning the room that gently
billow from second to second as wind comes in the
open window behind Hansen sitting in a lotus on the
couch: all of this a newness alien from the old of
surfboards and Goodwill mattresses on the bare floors
and surf pictures on the walls of the old surfhouse
where he lived while going to school when Hansen
two years ago, age eighteen, first came on the scene
having left his parents' home and moved in (that
surfhouse gone now in an urban renewal project
that in a year would not only have demolished the
row of similar houses on Ventura Point but will,
because of a long, high, stone and steel and concrete
seawall, outrider of a planned six story concrete and

96

palm surrounded resort hotel, destroy the rock and
sand formations of an ancient rivermouth made
point-break, a peeling symmetrical surf break that
provides on a strong west swell power rides up to an
eighth of a mile long, waves that give the rider an
ecstatic pride in his own courage in riding them;
rides that Gray feels are the major accomplishments of
an already long athletic career; rides that so far are
the best moments of his life), seeking, Gray felt,
his friendship, his approval: all of this a newness
overlaid by one other impression: the hypodermic
syringe lying on the white of Hansen's kitchen sink;
hearing now Hansen speak in answer to his warning
about being hustled by queers while hitchhiking
north, hearing Hansen now say, "So, it's all the same,
man; it'd be a new trip," blinked, paused, got a
mindflash of darkness and the highway and some
forty-five year old fag unzipping Hansen's fly, and
then, suddenly, totally, finally (at once thinking of
Hansen's favorite saying: 'Whatever happens, man,
happens; it's all up to the stars.') understood him,
understood why he always fell off in hard sections of
hard waves, understood why he wasn't surfing anymore,
understood why he had gone AWOL, understood the
dope dealing, the turning on of his thirteen year
old brother, understood the syringe, understood exactly
where Hansen was; felt excited by the insight,
relieved of any further curiosity, and disgusted enough
to say:

"Well, man, we're going up to Stanley's if you want a ride to get you started and right now I'm going outside cause if the police are really coming it could be anytime and I sure as hell don't want to be here when they do."

"Wow, man!" said Hansen.

Hoefer, looking at Gray, said nothing.

Gray, wanting somehow to undo the harshness of his own statement, looked up out the window, looked back at Hansen, then picked up the binoculars off the couch and brought them up to his eyes, looking beyond two blocks of tract housing, a field, the grey ribboned freeway, focusing them on the surf at the pier, then refocusing them for distance on California Street, seeing moving into clarity off the dark brown of the upper parking lot beyond the two squat silver Shell Oil storage tanks the long greygreen walls, six, seven, eight, more stacked out toward the horizon, the first good wave breaking maybe two hundred yards out across the high tide, its face a solid six foot, maybe seven, but too much wind, way too much, sections pushing over everywhere along its line. Gray jumped to the fourth wave, still smooth looking, a good five-footer starting to peak over, made the opening turn, stayed high in the pocket by the white now breaking, then drove down the green and out, setting up to make a hard turn back up. The long bulging wall ahead collapsed, turning over into whitewater.

"Stanley's is the only place," Gray said, looking
back at Hansen, seeing Hansen smiling, thinking then
'he's freaked out,' seeing Hansen's indian moccasins,
his rotten levis laden with iron-on patches, the faded
cloth a soft white-blue, the patches green, jean
blue, dark blue, wheat, black, solid over both knees
and up the thighs, pants Gray thought of as part of
Hansen's new doper style (but not that, not style in
the usual mode of unusual dress for gaining attention
but a style pronounced by a girl at a recent party,
saying: 'Those are your *soul* pants, right?' 'Yeah, right,
Hansen had said, liking her, liking that she had defined
it for him, seeming to know that he had *created*
the pants: had washed and sewed and ironed them:
had ironed then sewed on each patch actually working
on them everywhere in town: had slowly welded
and pressed them into his psyche under a variety of
mostly steamirons everywhere, Grandma's, Mom's,
a girl's named Lana, even Gray's new place: with each
new tear had ironed on patch after patch after patch
until, simply, they weren't cloth pants any longer
but were flesh, his flesh), pants that didn't fit with
the athletic look of the hard, tan belly and chest and
shoulders, pants that were one more bad omen for
Hansen's future, pants that matched the ruined,
blood reddened whites of Hansen's eyes now looking
into his; Gray thinking then 'what a handsome guy,
what a dumb fuck, why feel sorry for that'; then looked
at Hoefer sitting impassively in the armchair, running

his hand through his beard, obviously not seeing
that Hansen was simply fucked. 'Why,' Gray thought,
'even bother talking with the guy? If he doesn't
care, he doesn't care.'

"I'll be down in a minute," said Hoefer, seeing
that Gray was asking him to leave.

"Okay," Gray said. He tossed the binoculars next
to Hansen, glanced at a dayglo orange and soft pink
bordered black poster of a tall, skull grinning, white
skeleton draped in a garland of roses announcing THE
GRATEFUL DEAD, AVALON, SAN FRANCISCO,
thought symbolically 'that figures' and said:

"See you, Hans."

"Okay," Hansen answered.

As Gray turned and walked out the door, twisting
to avoid the last scarf, looking ahead to the dark well
of carpeted stairway going down to the street,
sensing the age and decay of the house, remembering
then not clearly the visual picture (the slowness of
it, the absolute concentration, the pulling of the
red into thin clean glass then the gentle, steady,
perfect push back) but thinking mostly of the shock
he had felt when watching one of Hansen's new
buddies shoot trancs at a party a week ago, remembering
how the kid (another guy that wasn't surfing much
anymore) had smiled afterward, softly, quietly, some
kind of weirdly beautiful light in his eyes, not
looking up at Gray, it seemed, although his eyes had
been fixed on him, but seeming to be looking up at

100

something else, someone else directly behind Gray, although there had been no one there, Hoefer sighed and Gray, hearing him, thought 'what the hell is Hoefer going to do? there's nothing he can do.'

In a minute Gray was gone and Hansen, still grinning, shrugged and shook his head.

"Well," Hoefer said, "queers are a pretty strange trip, you know."

"Ah, I was just jiving," said Hansen. "What's his problem anyway?"

"I don't know."

"He really gets uptight sometimes," Hansen said.

"Well," said Hoefer, "not that it's any of my business but what's the deal on that needle? You use that thing?"

Hansen threw out his hands.

"Bad karma, man."

"Yeah, you're right."

"Sure," Hoefer said.

Hansen grinned.

"Listen, you ass, why don't you wait a couple of days? Com'on out to my place. We'll ride Rincon tomorrow when the tide's better."

"No, I better not."

"I can dig it," Hoefer said, deciding to leave. He stood up. "Seeing some country'll be good for you."

"Yeah," Hansen said, "and save my ass, too."

"It will."

"I know."

"Okay," Hoefer said.

"You want to share a number before you split?"

"Well," Hoefer laughed, "sure." He sat down. "Gray brought me up here to get you off the dope, you know."

"Well," Hansen said, "the dope."

"The dope," Hoefer laughed, "sure."

Hansen got up, going past into the kitchen. Hoefer heard the oven door open, close.

"Your stash in there?"

"Part of it," Hansen said. He came back in carrying a cellophane bag of dark, wet-looking grass. "The rest is up in Santa Barbara. You want this stuff? It doesn't taste too good."

"No, not now."

"Yeah, take it, man. I'll put it out back. You can swing by later and pick it up."

"How much you want for it?"

"Nothing, man. It's a gift. I can't use it. I'm splitting for sure. It's jailtime around here, you know. I can't dig that. My name is on the list. I've got to go."

"Well," Hoefer said, "yeah, wow, okay. Where'll you put it?"

Hansen was looking down into the bowl of a dark curved pipe. He didn't answer for a moment.

"Out by the fence. You know that chainlink fence by the freight office? I'll bury it there at the corner."

"Good," Hoefer said, watching Hansen push a finger down into the bowl.

"Here," Hoefer said, getting up. He struck a match and held it over the bowl.

Hansen inhaled, sucking the flame down.

"I'd heard that things were hot," Hoefer said, "no pun intended." He sat down next to Hansen. "I thought I'd come by and see what was going on." Then he laughed. "No, man, really, to get your new stick. Are you taking it? I mean you're not hitchhiking with it, are you?"

"Yeah," Hansen said, passing the pipe, speaking without letting out smoke, talking up against the top of his throat, "my little brother has it but go ahead. Tell him I said you could use it. You'll really dig on it."

"Good," Hoefer said. "It'll work good in this swell." He looked at the pipe in his hand. "Listen, man, what's with your needle trip, like I don't understand that."

"There's nothing," Hansen said, "it's just a thing like all the guys in the brig were on to it and this one guy from L.A. liked me so he gave me the spike, a totally spaced out dude, you know, it's no big thing."

"Okay," Hoefer said, taking a toke.

"It's cool," Hansen said. He took the pipe.

"I mean like it's a little scary, you know."

"Listen, Hoef," Hansen said, "I'm onto a good thing."

"Yeah?" said Hoefer, watching the side of Hansen's face, looking at his eyes.

"God," Hansen said, still not letting air out of his lungs. He considered that expression. "Yeah," he said.

"God?"

"God . . ." Hansen was saying again giving Hoefer
the pipe. Hoefer took another toke, closing his eyes at
the burn hitting the back of his throat, smelling the
sweet, harsh reek. ". . . like I think I got really close."

"Yeah?" Hoefer opened his eyes, letting out the
smoke, seeing no color, feeling the warmth, his
thought taken by God, the word, enjoying the word,
feeling from it a moment of sensation like a church
thought, the smoke rolling in his brain, the invisible
host, laughing at that pun, feeling that laugh as a
moment of quiet and calm that made things (now
looking past Hansen onto the rose color of a scarf
dappled with shadow and weight and space, feeling too,
the space between Hansen and the rose, both floating)
seem musical, full of wonder, near to that feeling,
the pure feeling that often sitting in his church
gave him . . ."

"I'm not thinking God thoughts at all now, man,"
Hansen said, "and it's a real bringdown, you know
what I mean? I mean there's this giant hassle at me
now so I've got to cool it for a while, right?"

"Yeah," Hoefer agreed, "that's right," thinking
'. . . yes, it is, it is a God feeling, it must be (at eighteen,
at his father's insistence, he had driven off the coast
to Utah and Brigham Young University, driven there
in a 56 Caddy powered 34 Ford Tudor with his
Velzy-Jacobs racked on the top, starting higher
education full of fear and rebellion, feeling ill-prepared

and stifled, wanting no more formal education now
that high school was over, not even wanting to see
what the University had to offer, hating first the climate
and then the rigidity of studying, feeling there was
little hope of success for him in either the temporal or
the spiritual world there, longing for the coast, the
sea, missing his true satisfaction: the pump and lift of
surf excitement shooting adrenalin into him seventy,
eighty times a day, and so left the first time he received
what he wanted, a failing grade on his first english
composition exam, this three weeks after he enrolled,
and came back to the coast to be tossed out of home,
then — he sold the car — going on his own, surfing
through that winter, ending at the sea's edge, living
under the Malibu Pier during the summer of 59,
beginning a career based on hundreds and thousands
of hours spent in the water: creator of the best rides
ever seen at Secos, and some at Malibu and Rincon
too: solitary, unique, magical performances, his whole
land appearance based on his role as a performer,
full hair and beard, shaggy cutoff sleeveless woman's
furcoat, flamboyant shirts and pants, never shoes, always
dark glasses: rides that made him a star in high
school auditorium sixteen millimeter surf movies,
earned him board endorsements and free trips to Hawaii
and always work in nearly any surfboard shop on the
California coast: rides that gave him for more than
nine years a strong sense of self-worth, this sense
arrogantly based, a complete hang-everything-else

sense, a sense necessary to develop his skill; and rides done on hundreds of days spent totally stoned, first smoking marijuana that first summer at Malibu, marijuana becoming both a sacrament of his free existence and part of his pre-performance ritual, then a part of the joy of riding: a way of taking himself into his own body; but then quit two years ago at the age of twenty-seven after being rejected in love, had turned back to the church and his family, started work fulltime, won the girl back, married her, then started again, even though he felt he shouldn't, because, as he told her, telling her this while he was stoned, she wasn't: '. . . a tool for seeing the divine, like out there now' — both of them standing together on the beach at Oil Piers looking out along the pier seeing a wave silently loom up under the strutwork, dark, then emerald green, taking in sunlight through the back, diffusing it, spreading it in a moving glow gliding steadily toward them, all translucent along its face, all green motion and form — 'I can feel the whole weight of that wave actually moving through my head, I mean feel it, its reality, and can merge into it become one with that moving part of the entire breathing apparatus of the planet . . .') the same feeling.' "You know, man," Hoefer said, "I get it in church. You ought to go to church with me. Why don't you?"

"I mean," Hansen said, "it was with my little brother, you know, like I'd dropped a tab and went out at C Street and Donny was out and we started paddling up

to Stables without saying anything, it was just like
that, we looked at one another and I went into it, like,
well . . . wow. . . ."

"Yeah," Hoefer said, giving the pipe back.

"You want some? I'll lay some on you."

"Acid?"

"Yeah."

"No, man," said Hoefer, "I already know, you see."
He shook his head at the offered pipe.

"You sure?"

"I know," Hoefer laughed. "That's what I said."

Hansen laughed. He took another toke off the pipe,
then dumped the ashes out the window. "Bye," he
said.

"Right," Hoefer laughed. "That's it, you know. It's
a groovy feeling."

"It was really beautiful," Hansen said, "like all I
had to do was remember, you know, just remember."

"So?"

"So?"

"So you didn't remember," Hoefer laughed.

"Right," Hansen laughed, both now laughing
together, Hansen at one time Hoefer's follower, a
would be surf mag, surf flick star, had wanted to
accomplish in two years what Hoefer had taken six
years to accomplish, had style, good wave judgment
but no ability to finish, had fallen off on critical waves
in three critical Single A contests and so decided
he had no gift, Hansen now in this easy laughter feeling

himself to be, for the first time, finally, Hoefer's equal, and Hoefer feeling it too, both suddenly happy in their new understanding of each other.

"But I'll get it again," Hansen said, "I will."

Outside, Gray sat in Hoefer's paneltruck, feet up on the dash, idly watching the afterwork traffic. The freeway entrance three blocks ahead was jammed and two rows of cars were slowly rolling past the panel, feeding into the entrance. Gray was thinking about Stanley's, wondering what kind of shape its wave would have, wondering whether the swell was too big for it, and thinking about Stanley's took him into thinking about Hansen just as he saw Hoefer come out on the porch of the house, now remembering carrying his board up the rocks remembering that that had been a high tide day too with the outside reef pumping out at least a steady seven foot with super hairy almost inside-out body breaking rides, the last one sucking out so bad that sand off the bottom was coming up the wall then everything exploding under him and after dragging himself in, body banged up, legs shaky going up the rocks, yet excited about the ride, there was Hansen, AWOL, sitting inside the car, a dark blue navy coat draped over his head covering his face; and, after sliding the board in the trunk, then getting in, saying hello, through the coat Hans said: 'Hello, Chuck,' and all the way into town neither moved nor said more and only when they

reached the point and the old house had Gray seen
Hansen's face and shaved slick as an egg, sunburned,
peeling head (done by the screws at Long Beach
Naval Station Brig), a laughable contrast from his
former full sunbleached blond surfer's natural . . .

"Sorry, man," Hoefer said, opening the door. He had
his dark glasses on.

"What did he say?"

"Nothing," putting the key in the ignition.

"He say anything about the syringe?"

"Nope," Hoefer said, "I didn't push anything,"
looking in the sidemirror. Cars moved slowly across
the glass. He started the engine.

"He's going to blow his mind up one of these
days," Gray said.

"Well," Hoefer said, "maybe that's what he needs."

"Ha," Gray said, "you know he's a pretty damn
good surfer when he wants to be."

"I haven't really watched him," Hoefer said.

"He's not as good as you but he's pretty, you know.
I mean he has a good style, kind of like Mickey's."

There was an opening in the near lane and Hoefer
let out the clutch, easing them into the traffic.

"You know," Gray said, "Deese has a kind of funny
theory about Hans. Deese says everyone is born with
a guardian angel, like, and he says Hans lost his a
long time ago."

"Wow!" Hoefer laughed. He looked at Gray. Gray
was grinning. Still laughing, Hoefer reached under the

dash, clicking a plastic cartridge into the tapedeck. Instantly, madrigal voices singing *Lucy in the Sky with Diamonds* filled the air.

"The Beatles are too much," Hoefer laughed, looking back at the road. The lane was open ahead and Hoefer shifted into second and then high, looking again over at Gray. Gray was slumped back, beating out the time on his thighs. Hoefer wondered who Gray's angel was.

Home

"No," he said. He got up. She watched him chewing and swallowing, walking off. He forgot the check and came back. She pushed it to him. He looked at her.

"I'm coming," she said. "I'm the best man," he said. "I truly am. I truly love you." "I know you do," she said.

"You're not happy," he said. "Please, David," she said. She stood up, then walked on ahead.

He paid the check and they went outside. "God," he said, "I can't believe it; it just isn't true! It can't be true! Do you know what this means? Do you?" He started to cry. They walked along the long windows of the restaurant.

She started to touch him then didn't. "I know what you want," she said, "but I don't know if I can feel that way again."

"The truth," he said, "just tell me the truth."

"I really don't," she said. Then she said, "There is no truth."

"Jesus!" he said. "What is happening to me? I'm crying, for christ's sakes; I'm goddamn crying!"

They were at the car. He opened her door. "You cried the time you asked for a divorce," she said, "the time right after you married me."

"I know," he said. "I remember. Here. Take the keys. I'm going to walk."

"No," she said, "don't be ridiculous."

"I can't stay where I'm not loved," he said. "I won't." He was looking down at the asphalt of the parking lot.

"No," she said bitterly, "I suppose not. I suppose you can't."

He looked up at her. "I can't," he said.

"Do what you want," she said. "You always have. Do anything. I'm tired. I'm going home."

He looked at her. She didn't move. He looked down at his shoes. "Good Christ," he said.

The Uses of the Past

She had long straight brown hair and a face like
a child's, a gentle face. As they danced he told her she
looked like his first wife, a beautiful girl. She seemed
flattered and said that was nice and funny too because
for some reason she felt like his first wife, like they
were married.

When they left the bar they went home to her
apartment. They shared a number she had and went
to bed and for a moment he thought she was his first
wife and said so but she didn't mind and told him to
relax, just let things happen. He tried to and wanted to
but he couldn't, it wasn't any use, her body wouldn't
fit his, it wasn't the same.

Afterwards she brought him a drink but he got up
and dressed, saying he was sorry but he couldn't stay,
did she mind, could he call her, he really did like
her. She said yes, call anytime, and she wrote him out
the number but he never did.

Thirty

"Do you think there's someone like that? I mean someone who would know how to be with me when they were with me? That's not being sentimental, is it? I mean someone who really wanted what I have to give. That's not too much to ask, is it? I mean they wouldn't have to stay or anything. I'm not silly enough to ask that. I mean I'm not the only woman in the world, am I. I certainly don't think that."

Dale Herd, born 1940, is from Marcus, Washington. He was educated in Washington and California. *Early Morning Wind,* started in the fall of 68 in Carpinteria, California, was completed in Seattle, Washington, winter of 1970.